THIS WALKER BOOK BELONGS TO:

_____

_____

_____

To Cher,
nice save.

**WALKER BOOKS**
AND SUBSIDIARIES
LONDON • BOSTON • SYDNEY • AUCKLAND

First published in Great Britain 2008 by Walker Books Ltd
87 Vauxhall Walk, London SE11 5HJ

First published in the United States 2006 by Hyperion Books for Children.
British Publication Rights arranged with Sheldon Fogelman Agency, Inc.

10 9 8 7 6 5 4 3 2 1

© 2006 Mo Willems

The right of Mo Willems to be identified as author/illustrator of this work has been asserted by him
in accordance with the Copyright, Designs and Patents Act 1988

This book has been typeset in Cafeteria.

Printed in China

British Library Cataloguing in Publication Data:
a catalogue record for this book is available from the British Library

ISBN 978-1-4063-1229-4

www.walkerbooks.co.uk

# Edwina

## The Dinosaur Who Didn't Know She Was Extinct

Words and Pictures by

## Mo Willems

Everyone in town
knew Edwina.

She was the dinosaur who played with the neighbourhood kids.

She was the dinosaur who did favours for anyone who asked.

Edwina helped little old ladies cross the road.

And she baked chocolate-chip cookies for everyone.

Reginald knew just about everything about just about everything. He liked to give reports in class about all the things he knew.

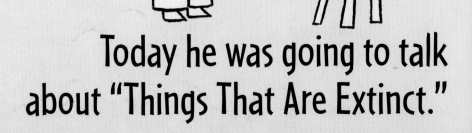

Today he was going to talk about "Things That Are Extinct."

But as soon as Reginald started, Beth McFeeder asked, "What about Edwina? She's a dinosaur."

Then Tommy Britcher said, "Yeah, Edwina can't be extinct. She bakes chocolate-chip cookies for us!"

Before he knew it, everyone except Reginald was outside, eating cookies.

No one listens to me with that dinosaur around! thought Reginald.

Well, tomorrow I'll prove to the whole town that dinosaurs really *are* extinct and – *POOF!* – Edwina will disappear!

The next morning, Reginald handed out flyers that made excellent arguments about how extinct dinosaurs are.

They also made excellent hats.

When flyers didn't work, Reginald tried protesting.

When protesting didn't work, he tried everything he could think of.

But no one listened.

Finally, Reginald broke down and cried. "Boohoo!" he sobbed. "WHY WON'T ANYONE LISTEN TO ME!?"

"I'll listen to you," said a voice from behind him.

Reginald took Edwina to his classroom.

Inside, Edwina listened as Reginald told her
the truth about dinosaurs.

He was persuasive.

He was expressive.

He was loud.

He was very
convincing.

Edwina was shocked.

When he had finished, Reginald felt fantastic!
No one had ever listened to him so well for so long.

Everything Reginald had said made sense. There was no doubt about it in Edwina's mind: she knew she was extinct.

She just didn't care.

**And, by then ...**

...neither did Reginald Von Hoobie-Doobie.

The End

# Mo Willems

Described by the *New York Times* as "the biggest new talent to emerge thus far in the '00s",
**Mo Willems** has been awarded two Caldecott Honors for his bestselling books *Don't Let the Pigeon Drive the Bus*
and *Knuffle Bunny*, and has won six Emmy Awards for his writing on *Sesame Street*.
He is also the creator of Cartoon Network's *Sheep in the Big City*. Mo lives with his family in Brooklyn, New York.

ISBN 978-1-84428-545-7

ISBN 978-1-4063-0812-9

ISBN 978-1-84428-513-6

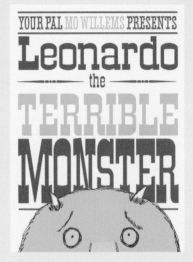

ISBN 978-1-4063-1215-7

ISBN 978-1-84428-059-9

ISBN 978-1-4063-1382-6

ISBN 978-1-4063-0158-8

*Available from all good booksellers*